Welcome to The GROW & READ Early Reader Program!

The GROW & READ book program was developed under the supervision of reading specialists to develop kids' reading skills while emphasizing the delight of storytelling. The series was created to help children enjoy learning to read and is perfect for shared reading and reading aloud.

These GROW & READ levels will help you choose the best book for every reader.

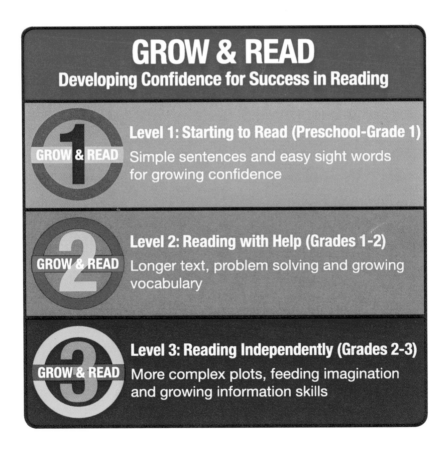

GROW & READ
Developing Confidence for Success in Reading

Level 1: Starting to Read (Preschool-Grade 1)
Simple sentences and easy sight words for growing confidence

Level 2: Reading with Help (Grades 1-2)
Longer text, problem solving and growing vocabulary

Level 3: Reading Independently (Grades 2-3)
More complex plots, feeding imagination and growing information skills

For more information visit growandread.com.

Published by Fabled Films LLC, New York

ISBN: 978-1-944020-23-1

Library of Congress Control Number: 2018960142

First Edition: April 2019

1 3 5 7 9 10 8 6 4 2

Cover Designed by Jaime Mendola-Hobbie
Jacket & Interior Art by Josie Yee
Interior Book Design by Aleks Gulan
Typeset in Stemple Garamond, Mrs. Ant and Pacific Northwest
Printed by Everbest in China

FABLED FILMS PRESS
NEW YORK CITY
fabledfilms.com

For information on bulk purchases for promotional use, please contact Consortium Book Sales & Distribution Sales department at ingrampublishersvcs@ingramcontent.com or 1-866-400-5351.

The
Chestnut Challenge

by

Tracey Hecht

Illustrations by
Josie Yee

Fabled Films Press
New York

Chapter 1

The sky was dark.

The stars were sparkling.

Many animals were sleeping,
but three friends were wide awake.

They were playing a game of
chestnut checkers!

"Tobin, it's your move,"
the sugar glider said.

He snapped his small fingers.

He tapped his tiny foot.

"Hurry up!"
the sugar glider chided.

"Bismark," the fox said.

"Let Tobin take his time.

Deciding which chestnut to move is not easy."

"Oh goodness!" Tobin sighed.

The pangolin scratched his chin.

The pangolin chewed his claw.

Finally, Tobin moved a chestnut.

"Ah-ha! You have fallen into my trap!" Bismark said.

"I will be the chestnut champion now! Watch this!"

Bismark moved one of his chestnuts.

"But Bismark," Tobin said,
"now I can do this."

Tobin jumped a chestnut across the board—
and captured all of Bismark's chestnuts!

"Chirping chickadees!" Bismark cried.

"I am not a chestnut champion.

I am a loser.

A failure.

A flop!"

"Oh Bismark." Tobin laughed.

"You are too serious about chestnuts.

It is only a game."

"ONLY A GAME ?"

a voice called from the shadows.

"NOT TO THIS CHAMPION !"

Chapter 2

"Hello, chums!" a chinchilla said.
"I am Chandler.

The real chestnut champion!"

The chinchilla was one cheeky chap.

Bismark scrunched his nose.

"I am not sure we should play
with this chinchilla,"
Bismark whispered to his friends.

"He seems a bit **braggy**.

A bit **boastful**."

"Bismark," Dawn said.

"Let's give him a chance.

Chandler," Dawn said to the chinchilla.

"Which one of us would you like to play?"

Chandler picked
up a chestnut.

Chandler tossed
the chestnut
from paw to paw.

Chandler placed the
chestnut on the board.

"I choose him!"

Chandler pointed to Tobin.

"I challenge your champion
to a competition!"

Chapter 3

"Oh dear," Tobin said.

"But I don't like competitions.

I play for fun."

"Come on, Tobin!"
Bismark cheered his friend.

"Show this chinchilla who
the real champion is!"

"Tobin," Dawn said.
"It is your choice if you want to play."

"Enough chitchat!"
Chandler interrupted.

"Do you accept my challenge or not?"

Tobin looked at Dawn.

Tobin looked at Bismark.

Tobin took a deep breath.

"Okay," Tobin said.

"I will play. But just for fun."

Chapter 4

Chandler and Tobin started to play.

Chandler's brow wrinkled.

Tobin's jaw tightened.

No one seemed to be having fun.

Suddenly, Chandler gasped!

"Look over there!" Chandler cried out.

Chandler pointed to something behind the three friends.

Dawn, Tobin, and Bismark all turned.

And that's when Chandler
reached forward—

and **moved** one of Tobin's chestnuts!

Dawn was confused.

"I didn't see anything unusual over there," Dawn said.

"Nada, nothing!" Bismark added.

"Chandler the Chinchilla, you need to get your eyes checked!"

"Maybe it was just a shadow. Sorry.

But it's my turn. And Tobin, my chap—

your chestnut is now mine!"

Chandler captured the chestnut
that he had just moved!

Dawn leaned over.

Dawn studied the board.

Dawn did not remember
Tobin's chestnut being in that spot.

"Amigo, pangolino!" Bismark cried.

"You cannot lose to this cheeky challenger!"

Tobin's heart beat faster.

Just then Chandler took a big, deep breath.

The chinchilla sneezed and
leaned over the board.

And when the friends were not looking—

Chandler moved two more chestnuts!

Chapter 5

"Excuse me!" Chandler sniffed.

Chandler let out a chuckle.

He was pleased.

No one had seen him cheating.

"Tobin," Bismark cried.

"It's your turn.

Don't let this chinchilla

turn you into a chestnut chump!"

Tobin closed his eyes to think.

And when Tobin's eyes were shut,

Chandler reached out . . .

and stole one of Tobin's chestnuts!

"Dawn, Tobin!" Bismark hollered.

"Did you see that?

This chinchilla is not only

cheeky–he's sneaky!

Chandler just stole Tobin's chestnut!"

Chandler's mouth dropped open.

"Who me?"
Chandler said.

"But my sugar glider chap,
you must be mistaken."

Dawn took a step forward.

She had seen Chandler take
Tobin's chestnut, too.

"Chandler," Dawn said.
"Are you sure you didn't take
one of Tobin's chestnuts?"

Dawn held Chandler in her gaze.

Chandler's cheeks became pink.

Chandler's teeth started to chatter.

And then, from Chandler's paw,

out dropped the chestnut!

Chapter 6

Chandler coughed.

Chandler cried out.

And then, Chandler caved.

"Yes!" Chandler said.

"I am not a chestnut champion.

I am a cheater."

"Chandler," Dawn said.

"Champions don't play cheap tricks."

"And besides," Tobin added.

"Playing chestnuts is not about winning.

It's about having fun and doing your best."

"I should not have cheated," Chandler said.

"But I wanted to be the champion.

I wanted to win."

"Chandler," Tobin said.

"No one wins every time.

But the more you practice,

the better you'll play."

Dawn smiled at the chinchilla.

"Chandler," Dawn said.

"Would you like a second chance?"

Tobin clapped.
"Yes, I will cheer you along!"

Bismark narrowed his eyes.
"And I will keep an eye on your chestnuts!"

And so the four friends settled into a

cheerful game of chestnut checkers.

Grow & Read Storytime Activities
For The Nocturnals Early Reader Books!

Download Free Printables:

Sight Word Games

Brigade Mask Craft and Coloring Pages!

Visit **growandread.com**
#NocturnalsWorld

The NOCTURNALS

FUN FACTS!

What are The Nocturnal Animals?

Pangolin: The pangolin is covered with keratin scales on most of its body except its belly and face. A pangolin sprays a stinky odor, much like a skunk, to ward off danger. It then curls into a ball to protect against attack. Pangolins have long, sticky tongues to eat ants and termites. Pangolins do not have teeth.

Red Fox: The red fox has reddish fur with a big, bushy tail and a white tip. Red foxes are clever creatures with keen eyesight. They have large, upright ears to hear sounds far away.

Sugar Glider: The sugar glider is a small marsupial. It looks like a flying squirrel. It has short gray fur, black rings around its big eyes, and a black stripe that runs from its nose to the end of its tail. Sugar gliders have special skin that stretches from the ankle to the wrist. This special skin allows sugar gliders to glide from tree to tree to find food and escape danger.

Chinchilla: Chinchillas live in the mountains and have soft, dense fur that protects them from the cold. They have thick, bushy tails and resemble kangaroos, with front legs that are shorter than their back legs. Chinchillas are social animals that bark, chirp, and grunt to talk to their herd.

Nighttime Fun Facts!

Nocturnal animals are animals that are awake and active at night. They sleep during the day.

The chestnut, which is a fruit, has a green husk until it becomes ripe and turns brown. The Nocturnal Brigade uses them to play their favorite game: chestnut checkers.

About the Author

Tracey Hecht is a writer and entrepreneur who has written, directed and produced for film. She created a Nocturnals Read Aloud Writing Program in partnership with the New York Public Library that has expanded nationwide. Tracey splits her time between Oquossoc, Maine and New York City.

About the Illustrator

Josie Yee is an award-winning illustrator and graphic artist specializing in children's publishing. She received her BFA from Arizona State University and studied Illustration at the Academy of Art University in San Francisco. She lives in New York City with her daughter, Ana, and their cat, Dude.

About Fabled Films

Fabled Films is a publishing and entertainment company creating original content for young readers and middle grade audiences. Fabled Films Press combines strong literary properties with high quality production values to connect books with generations of parents and their children. Each property is supported with additional content in the form of animated web series and social media as well as websites featuring activities for children, parents, bookstores, educators and librarians.

fabledfilms.com

FABLED FILMS PRESS
NEW YORK CITY

Read All of The Grow & Read Nocturnal Brigade Adventures!

This series can help children enjoy learning to read and is perfect for shared reading and reading aloud.

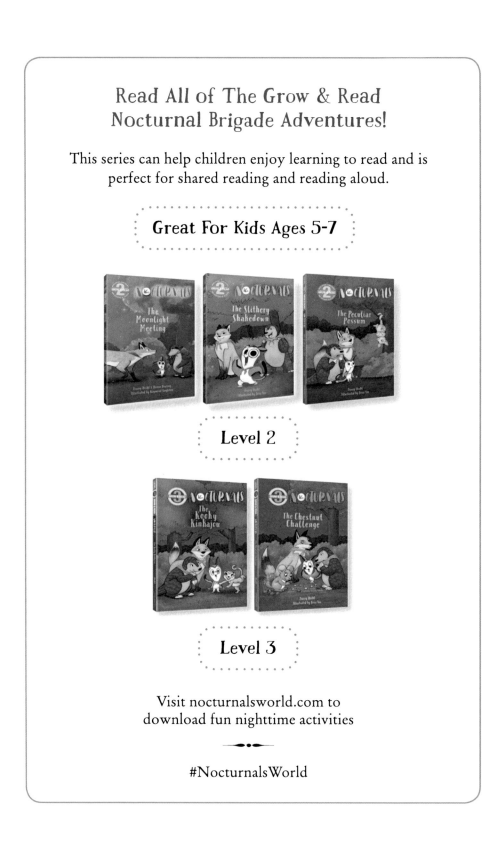

Level 2

Level 3

Visit nocturnalsworld.com to download fun nighttime activities

#NocturnalsWorld